THE STEADFAST TIN SOLDIER

RETOLD AND ILLUSTRATED BY

Rachel Isadora

G. P. PUTNAM'S SONS • NEW YORK

G. P. Putnam's Sons, a division of The Putnam & Grosset Group,

200 Madison Avenue, New York, NY 10016.

G. P. Putnam's Sons, Reg. U.S. Pat. & Tm. Off.

Published simultaneously in Canada.

Printed in Hong Kong by South China Printing Co. (1988) Ltd.

Designed by Donna Mark. Text set in Trump Mediaeval

Library of Congress Cataloging-in-Publication Data

Isadora, Rachel. The steadfast tin soldier /

retold and illustrated by Rachel Isadora.   p.   cm.

Summary: The perilous adventures of a toy soldier who loves a

paper dancing girl culminate in tragedy for both of them.

[1. Fairy tales. 2. Toys—Fiction.] I. Andersen, H. C. (Hans

Christian). 1805-1875. Standhaftige tinsoldat. English. II. Title.

PZ8.I84St   1996 [Fic.]—dc20   95-15816   CIP   AC

ISBN 0-399-22676-1

1   3   5   7   9   10   8   6   4   2

First Impression

And this one's for Brian

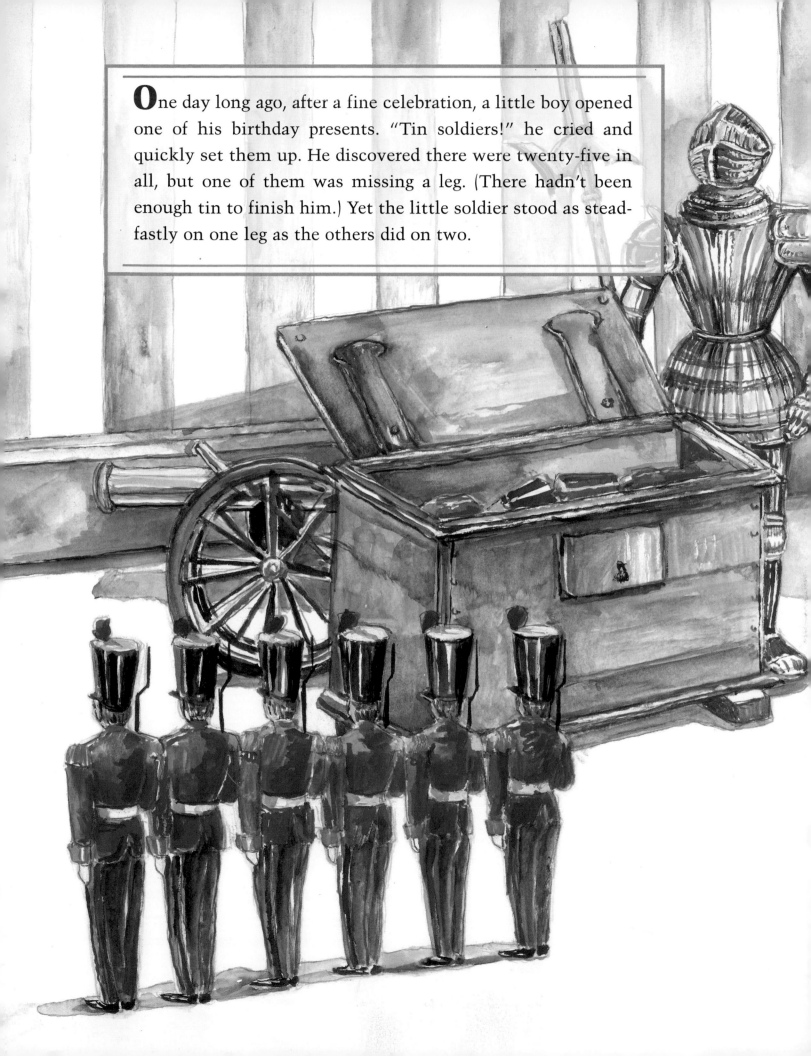

One day long ago, after a fine celebration, a little boy opened one of his birthday presents. "Tin soldiers!" he cried and quickly set them up. He discovered there were twenty-five in all, but one of them was missing a leg. (There hadn't been enough tin to finish him.) Yet the little soldier stood as steadfastly on one leg as the others did on two.

The first thing the tin soldier saw in the boy's room was a
cardboard castle with a lovely paper ballerina standing in the
doorway. Her dress was made of gauze, with a brilliant jewel
held in place by a blue sash. She stood poised on one leg, the
other lifted so high that the tin soldier thought she too had
only one leg. And the steadfast tin soldier fell instantly
in love.

Later that evening, when the tin soldiers were put back in their box and everyone was sound asleep, the toys began to play. Only the steadfast tin soldier and the pretty little ballerina remained in place. He never took his eyes off her, as she balanced so steadily on the tip of her toe.

Then the clock struck midnight. A lid flew up—*bang!*—and out sprang a goblin.

"Tin soldier, keep your eyes to yourself!" the goblin cried out.

But the tin soldier pretended not to hear and kept looking at the ballerina.

"Just you wait until tomorrow!" the goblin warned.

In the morning, the boy awoke and put the tin soldier on the windowsill. When he turned away, a gust of wind (or was it the goblin?) blew the tin soldier out the window. He landed on the street below, his bayonet stuck between two cobblestones.

The boy and the housekeeper rushed down to find him, but they passed by without seeing him. (The tin soldier thought it improper for one in uniform to shout.) Soon it began to rain, so the boy and the housekeeper went back inside.

When the rainstorm was over, two boys came walking by and spotted the tin soldier.

"Look! Let's see what kind of sailor he makes."

They made a boat out of newspaper, put the tin soldier on board, and sent him racing down the gutter in a stream of rain-water. The boat tossed and turned. The tin soldier felt seasick, but he remained standing steadfast on his one leg.

Suddenly, the boat was swept under a plank covering the gutter, and everything went black.

Out popped a tremendous water rat.

"You must pay the toll!" the rat declared. "You must pay the toll!"

But the tin soldier, frightened as he was, stood steadfast, looking ahead, saying nothing. The boat rushed on, and the rat raced after it, gnashing his teeth furiously.

The current moved faster and faster toward a patch of daylight. But just when the tin soldier was hopeful, the current hurled the boat over the edge and sent it crashing down into the grand canal. The tin soldier stood at attention as the boat whirled round and round, filling up with water. He was up to his neck when the newspaper fell apart, and down he went. All he could think of was the lovely ballerina he would never see again.

No doubt he would have ended up in the mud at the bottom of the canal if a fish hadn't swum by and swallowed him up.

Inside the fish, he found himself in the darkest place of all. But the tin soldier lay there steadfast, even when the fish began to twist and thrash about in the most terrifying way.

After what seemed the longest time, the tin soldier saw a sudden flash of daylight and heard a voice cry, "A tin soldier!" He couldn't have known, but the fish had been caught, taken to market, sold, and brought back to the very same house in which the boy lived. In the kitchen, the cook had sliced it open.

After dinner, the housekeeper found the tin soldier and took him up to the boy's room. How pleased and surprised everyone was to see this remarkable fellow who had come home in the belly of a fish. The tin soldier was not proud in the least. He was only amazed and so happy to find himself back in the room with the lovely ballerina.

There she was, still balanced on one leg just as he had left her. He was so touched that she had remained steadfast, he would have shed tin tears had he not been in uniform. He looked at her, and she at him, neither saying a word.

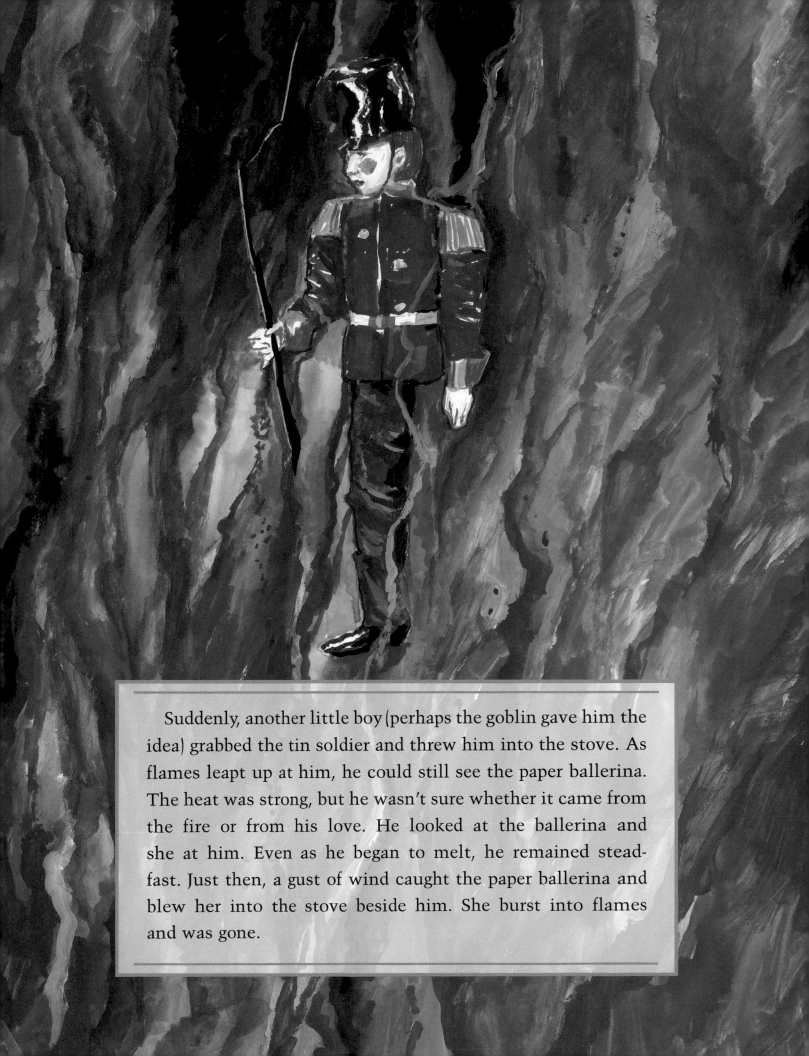

Suddenly, another little boy (perhaps the goblin gave him the idea) grabbed the tin soldier and threw him into the stove. As flames leapt up at him, he could still see the paper ballerina. The heat was strong, but he wasn't sure whether it came from the fire or from his love. He looked at the ballerina and she at him. Even as he began to melt, he remained steadfast. Just then, a gust of wind caught the paper ballerina and blew her into the stove beside him. She burst into flames and was gone.